VANUK VANUK

Story by Guido Sperandio
Pictures by Piero Ventura
Translated by Jane Murgo

DOUBLEDAY & COMPANY, INC.
GARDEN CITY, NEW YORK

ISBN: 0-385-01161-X Trade
0-385-07382-8 Prebound
Library of Congress Catalog Card Number 73-79711
Copyright © 1973 by G. Sperandio and P. Ventura
All Rights Reserved
Printed in the United States of America
First Edition

. . . and this is the village of the Quanta, a village where life was both peaceful and happy.

Until one day . . .

. . . BOC!

A violet point appeared from the ground and blossomed
so rapidly that it lifted up both people and things.

Just like that, the Quantimonio burst into bloom.

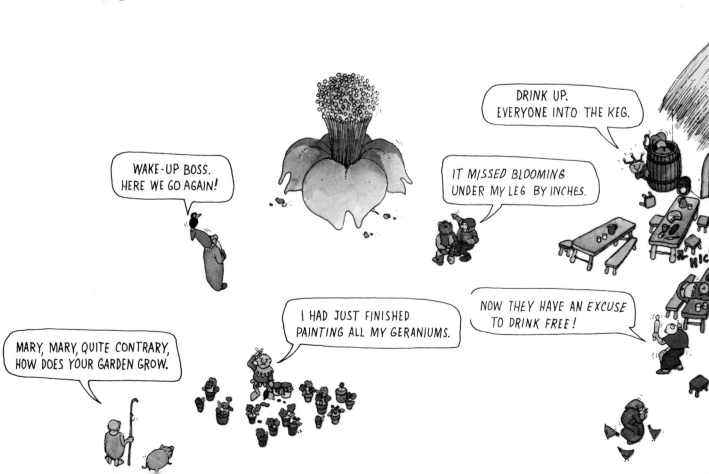

BUT WHAT IS QUANTIMONIO?

SEEDS OF THE QUANTIMONIO.

LEAVES OF THE QUANTIMONIO.

The Quantimonio, a flower belonging to the tubular-dynamic species, grows only in one place, a place which does not appear on any map: the village of the Quanta.

Despite extensive research, the causes of its bloom remain a mystery. Metlicoviz, a world-renowned authority on the subject, describes it as a rare flower of exotic and luminous colors with large, fleshy petals. Its aspect, he says, is both fascinating and horrifying.

SOUNDS OF THE QUANTIMONIO
BURSTING FORTH FROM THE GROUND.

The Quantimonio appears without warning. Within a half hour it is full grown, complete with petals, leaves and corolla. It reaches a height of nearly 25 feet.

Those who have seen it grow will never forget it.

The sudden eruption of the Quantimonio makes it frightening to the Quanta, but very appetizing to those known as the Sacripanti.

(from *Flowers and Fauna of Your Country*, by permission of the publisher)

The Quantimonio had hardly bloomed before the
Sacripanti spotted it. From their dark and
gloomy castle on top of the mountain, they could see
all that happened in the village of the Quanta.

At the first "BOC," the Sacripanti mounted their horses
and charged into the valley.

THEY'RE
COMING!

In a flash the Quanta abandoned their village.
In a flash the Sacripanti invaders struck.
They pulled up every Quantimonio to the last root.
They emptied houses, chicken coops and stables.

What they could not carry away, they destroyed.

BUT WHO ARE SACRIPANTI

SACRIPANTI AT THE MOMENT OF BIRTH.

ADULT SACRIPANTI IN TYPICAL ANTI-ATOMIC ARMOR.

The Sacripanti are a people who have been noted from the time of antiquity for their warlike nature and their love of destruction.

Defeated and held back by the Roman legions, the Sacripanti are minutely described in the chronicles of the time.

Over the course of centuries, their exploits have become well known throughout the continent of Europe.

PANZER-SACRIPANTI.

SACRIPANTI CHIEF IN HIS SUNDAY BEST - A SUPER CORKSCREW HELMET.

SACRIPANTI HELMET, WHICH PREVENTS
INDIVIDUAL THOUGHT AND REASON.

The Sacripanti exist in order to destroy. War is their only
pastime, profession and goal.

SACRIPANTI HELMET, WET.

Every Sacripanti is born wearing armor. This
armor is identical for all except the Chief,
who has an additional horn on his helmet.

EVERYDAY HELMET OF THE
SACRIPANTI CHIEF.

The Sacripanti do not think or reason and
therefore do not make decisions. Thinking is the
exclusive duty of their chief, who is the supreme
authority.

QUANTIMONIO BIRTHDAY CAKE.

What do the Sacripanti eat, drink, and wear?
Exclusively Quantimonio . . .
Which is also their medicine and the raw material for
everything they need and use.

* SWORD

SACRIPANTI DEFOLIATION BOOT WITH
BUILT-IN LAWN MOWER TOES.

QUANTIMONIO NATURALLY PRESERVED -
NET WEIGHT DRAINED 12 OUNCES.

The only person to remain in the village during the attack was the Blacksmith.

Naturally, he was well hidden . . . inside the foliage of a tree.

Upon seeing the last of the Sacripanti vanish, he climbed down and whistled. This was the signal.

The Quanta crept cautiously out from behind the bushes
of the surrounding hills and returned to what
had once been their pleasant village.

The Blacksmith scratched his head. It was his way of thinking. He then walked to the main square and whistled again. This was the signal for the Quanta to assemble. Everyone agreed that they must not allow the Sacripanti to devastate the village again.

Since the Sacripanti were so much stronger, it was necessary for the Quanta to find an ingenious . . .

As usual, it was the Blacksmith who had it.
As usual, it was the Blacksmith who carried it out.
And as usual, although everyone approved of the idea,
nobody could grasp what it was.

The Blacksmith took a piece of colored chalk and with an
air of determination started sketching strange lines on the ground.

He did not let any obstacle stand in his way—not
walls, or houses, or people, or animals.

Within a few hours, the whole village resembled a
blackboard at the end of an arithmetic lesson.

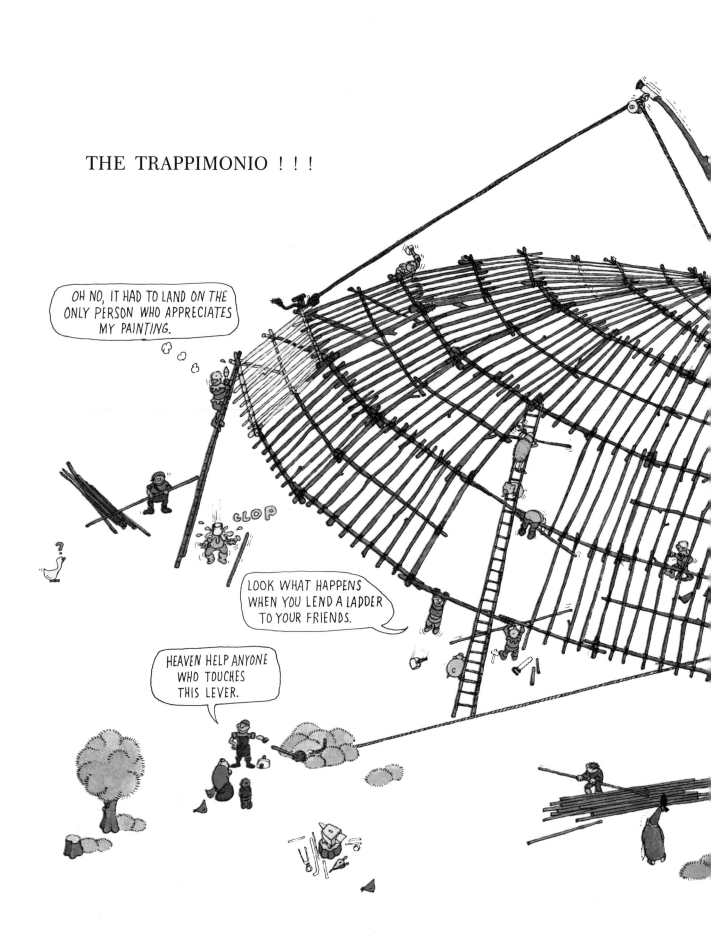

Instructions for Use of the Trappimonio
(according to the intentions of the inventor)

1. Keep the trap high off the ground.
2. Wait until the moment the Sacripanti are beneath it.
3. Then lower the lever swiftly.
4. The cable will release; the Trappimonio will fall,
   imprisoning every Sacripanti to the last man.

In time, the Quantimonio bloomed once more.

The Quanta hurried to put the final touches on the Trappimonio.

All except Vanuk, who in keeping with his nature continued to
follow the butterfly he had been chasing for four days, crying
"Vanuk, Vanuk."
(This was the only word he had ever been heard to utter and one
that, even in the language of the Quanta, had no meaning.)
It did not seem possible to him that the butterfly had finally
come to rest, unexpectedly, on a piece of brightly polished wood.

With all the strength of his body, Vanuk
threw himself upon it.

WHY ALWAYS ON
MY DAY OFF?

VAN..

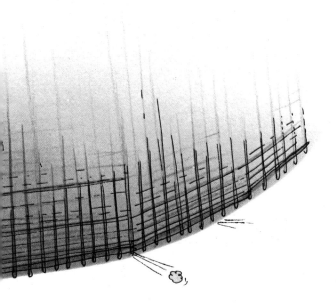

No words can describe what followed:

At the first touch of the lever, the gigantic Trappimonio crashed to the ground . . .

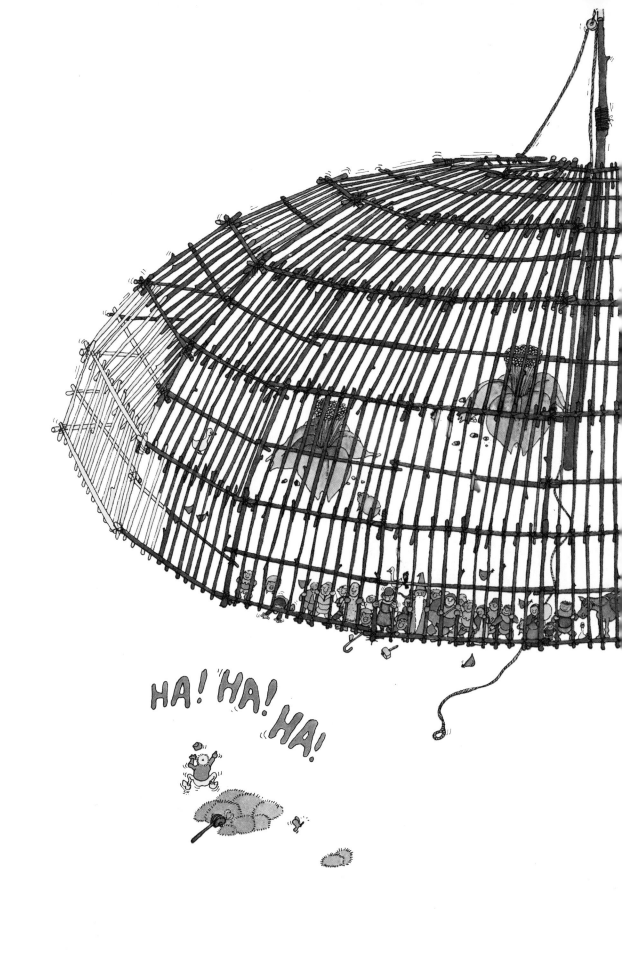

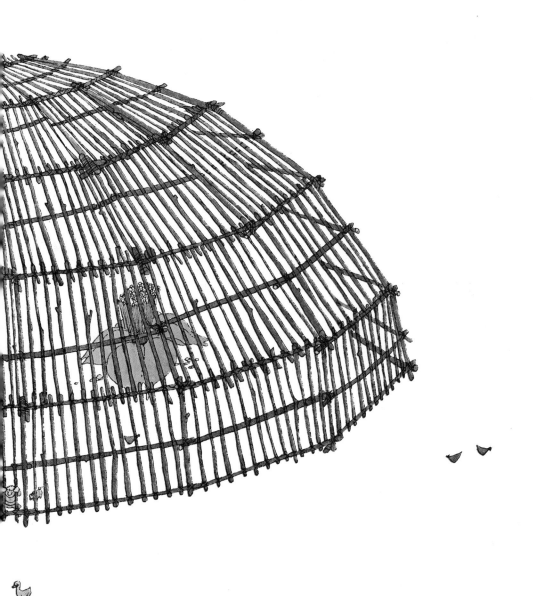

. . . imprisoning the entire population of the Quanta.

There followed a bleak silence, broken only by the carefree
laughter of Vanuk. Then came the clatter of
horses' hoofs. The sharp point of a lance appeared,
followed by one, two,
three, a hundred, a thousand Sacripanti.

The Quanta were helpless.

Only Vanuk remained to be captured.

Feeling the point of a lance pass through the cloth
of his pants, poor Vanuk couldn't suppress a desperate: "VAN . . .

. . . UK!" The Sacripanti stopped in their tracks, paralyzed, then astonished and finally terrified.

What had happened?

It seems that "Vanuk," in their language, meant:

VERBOTENMEINKAMPFKRANKENMITTELGENUNGVOLKS
PARTEIPFENNINGVONWURSTELGEGANGENZURUCK!

Though today no one understands the word's precise meaning, it was the most terrible and shocking thing that the ear of a Sacripanti could hear.

And so, a moment later, the Sacripanti abandoned the village of the Quanta and fled back to the mountain which they had just left with such pride and vain glory.

The Quanta couldn't believe that for the first time in their history they had achieved a victory over the Sacripanti.

The idea of a cake "as large as the main square of the village" was, naturally, the Blacksmith's.

And, naturally, the Quanta carried it out to the letter.

Except Vanuk, who still could not understand how he had passed so swiftly from the point of a lance to the creamy softness of a chocolate cake.